This book belongs to

Good Morning,

by CAROL VOTAW

illustrated by
SUSAN BANTA

Little Polar Bear

NORTHWORD
Minnetonka, Minnesota

The illustrations were created using acrylics on vellum surface Bristol
The text and display type were set in Big Caslon and Berkeley Oldstyle
Composed in the United States of America
Art directed and designed by Lois A. Rainwater
Edited by Kristen McCurry

Books for Young Readers

11571 K-Tel Drive
Minnetonka, MN 55343
www.tnkidsbooks.com

Library of Congress Cataloging-in-Publication Data

Votaw, Carol
Good morning, little polar bear / by Carol Votaw ; illustrated by Susan Banta.
p. cm.
ISBN 1-55971-932-X (hardcover)
1. Animals--Arctic regions--Juvenile literature. I. Banta, Susan, ill. II. Title.

QL105.V68 2005
591.7'0911'3--dc22   2005000328

Printed in Thailand
10 9 8 7 6 5 4 3 2 1

For Jeannie and Sarah,
who inspire me daily
—C.V.

To Michael, and to my amazing Mother
—S.F.B.

Good morning, little polar bear,
It's time for you to wake.
Stretch your frozen, furry paws
And give yourself a shake.

Good morning, little puffin,
It's time for you to fly.
The sun is just beginning
To paint the morning sky.

Good morning, little arctic fox,
It's time to go exploring.
Hush your noisy, wiggly nose,
Enough of all that snoring!

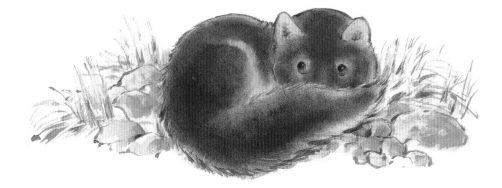

Good morning, little arctic hare,
It's time to hop about.
Come make a maze of snowy prints,
You furry, bunny scout!

Good morning, little arctic wolf,
It's time to leave your den.
Come join the playful, tumbling pups,
My sleepy, little friend.

Good morning, little walrus,
It's time to catch some sun.
Basking on the frozen beach
Can be a bunch of fun!

Good morning, little harp seal,
It's time to catch some fish.
You dive down for your breakfast
And eat without a dish.

Good morning, little narwhal,
It's time to squeal and click.
You wear a pretty icicle,
Now that's a fancy trick!

Good morning, little meadow vole,
It's time to join the race.
Your friends are on the tundra
Playing lively games of chase.

Good morning, little caribou,
It's time to move along.
The herd is up and running.
That's where you belong.

Good morning, little musk ox,
It's time, I think you know,
To shake your messy tangles
Full of sparkly winter snow.

Good morning, little snowy owl,
It's time for you to rise.
No more sleeping in for you.
Open wide your golden eyes.

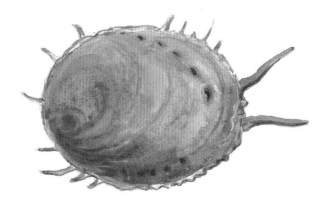

Good morning, little sea otter,
It's time to roll your bed.
Your hammock's made of floating kelp
And magic seaweed thread.

And you, my little love,
Peek from your snuggly place.
The sun is blowing kisses,
They're landing on your face.

Yes, you, my little love,
At last, the morning's come.
The stars are gone,
The sun is up.
It's time to have some fun!

ALL THE ANIMALS IN THIS BOOK MAKE THEIR HOME IN THE ARCTIC.

Polar Bear

Polar bears are the largest bears in the world. Some adult males weigh over 1,000 pounds. However, cubs weigh less than two pounds at birth. They are born hairless, blind, and deaf. Polar bear cubs stay with their mother in a snow den for three months.

Arctic Wolf

Wolves are social animals. They live in small family groups called packs. Both male and female wolves help care for pups. Arctic wolves also hunt in packs.

Puffin

Puffins dig burrows between rocks on steep cliffs. They build a nest at the end of the burrow and lay one egg each year. Puffins eat small fish. Their tongues have tiny, hook-like spines, allowing them to hold fish in their beak while diving underwater to catch even more fish.

Walrus

Walruses are related to seals and sea lions. Males weigh up to 2,000 pounds and must eat thousands of shellfish every day. Those long, funny whiskers help a walrus find food in deep, muddy water.

Arctic Fox

The arctic fox has white fur in the winter and grayish-brown fur in the summer. These colors help camouflage the fox from its predators and prey. When sleeping, the arctic fox curls its long, bushy tail around its body to stay warm. Even the nose and feet are tucked inside the cozy tail.

Harp Seal

Harp seals are born with a fluffy, white coat. This makes it difficult for predators to see them on the snow. Mother harp seals nurse their pups for only two weeks and then leave them. After that, the little seals must teach themselves to swim and catch fish.

Arctic Hare

Hares live in large groups. At a young age they learn to sit so still that predators can't see them. When they do move, their powerful hind legs allow them to run so fast that foxes and wolves have trouble catching them.

Narwhal

What looks like a long horn coming out of this arctic whale's head is actually a tooth. When male narwhals are one year old, their upper left tooth grows outward in a spiral. This tooth may grow ten feet long. Narwhals are noisy whales. They click, squeal, and whistle.

Meadow Vole

Meadow voles look like field mice. They are busy day and night. Meadow voles build nests in the shape of a ball. By chewing and trampling grass, they create a network of runways. During the winter, meadow voles continue to use these runways under the snow.

Caribou

Caribou shed their antlers every year. Unlike other deer, both males and females have large antlers. Caribou are strong swimmers. Their hollow hairs trap air to keep them warm and help them float in the water.

Musk Ox

The musk ox has long, shaggy hair, probably the longest hair found on any wild animal. Both male and female musk oxen have horns and are very protective of their young. When they sense danger, adults in the herd form a circle around the young with their horns facing outward.

Snowy Owl

The snowy owl is an unusual owl. Most owls hunt at night, but snowy owls hunt during the day. Snowy owls live where there are no trees so they are often seen sitting on the arctic ground, which is called the tundra. They even make their nests on the tundra.

Sea Otter

Sea otters love to play. They do not have blubber to keep warm like seals and walruses do. Instead, they have very dense fur. Abalone is their favorite food. Sea otters are one of the few animals that use tools. While floating on their backs, they use small rocks to crack abalone shells. At night sea otters tie kelp around themselves so they don't float away as they sleep.

CAROL VOTAW earned a B.A. from St. Mary's College, where she studied history, art, and music, and an M.B.A. from Indiana University. She has worked in advertising and now writes children's stories and teaches piano. Carol lives in Rochester Hills, Michigan, with her husband and two daughters. She enjoys kayaking, sailing, and skiing with her family. *Good Morning, Little Polar Bear* is her first book.

SUSAN BANTA was born in Washington D.C. but grew up in Montreal, Canada. She earned a degree in fine arts from Syracuse University and she survived careers in several design fields, including fashion illustration, layout, and graphics production (which involved a lot of rubber cement). She has illustrated lots of educational materials, and close to thirty books.

Susan and her husband, a retired librarian, now live in Brookfield, Vermont. When not at the drawing board, she likes to read, quilt, garden, snow-shoe, and cross-country ski.

Let's go have some fun!